by ALICE FAYE DUNCAN

Miss Viola
and Uncle Ed Lee

illustrated by CATHERINE STOCK

ATHENEUM BOOKS for YOUNG READERS

For Ms. Lucinda McGee
and Mr. Lonnie Jackson,
my senior buddies who
have shared their stories.
A. F. D.

For
Maureen
Cynnie
Eve
Norman
John
Sandi
Toni
Peter
Gerard
Douglas
Wendy
and Angie
with love and thanks
C. S.

This is a story about Miss Viola and Uncle Ed Lee. They used to be my neighbors when I lived on Joubert Street.

Miss Viola lived on my right in a little lavender house. It had bright white shutters and a white picket fence. Her yard was always cut. Her shrubs were always trimmed, 'cause Miss Viola was a neat woman. She kept her place clean.

Uncle Ed Lee lived on my left in a little red house. It had hanging black shutters and a leaning mailbox. He had a rusty wire fence. His grass was always tall, 'cause Uncle Ed Lee was a trifling old man. He could be lazy to the core.

One Saturday, I went to visit old Uncle Ed Lee.
We played checkers, my favorite game, and we
ate popsicles under his big shade tree.

While I studied the checker board, trying my best to win, Uncle Ed Lee watched Miss Viola pruning the roses in her garden.

He watched her sweep her porch.

He watched her paint
her fence.

He watched her mow her grass that was
always green and pretty.
"Bradley," he said, "Miss Viola is so neat.

Have you ever noticed her spotless place?
Have you ever noticed that her grass stays
cut? And her fence stays sparkling white."

Of course I heard Uncle Ed Lee, but I was trying to focus on the game. So I covered my ears, to give him a hint, but he still would not be quiet.

Uncle Ed Lee kept talking all about Miss Viola.

"Have you ever noticed her bright smile?" he asked. "Have you ever noticed that she don't cuss or fight? Miss Viola is sweet! She's neat. And I'm gonna make her a friend of mine."

"A friend of yours?" I said. "You and Miss Viola?!" I fell out of the chair from laughing 'cause that was a kooky combination.

"Uncle Ed Lee," I said, "You can't be buddies with a lady like that. Look at her. Look at you! Y'all are totally different."

"We are," agreed Uncle Ed Lee. "I am junky as a pack rat. Miss Viola is neat as a pin. But just because folks are different, don't mean they can't be friends."

Uncle Ed Lee had a point. What he said was very true. So I brushed myself off and I walked over to see how Miss Viola felt.

"How you doing?" I asked Miss Viola. "I've got something on my mind. Uncle Ed Lee from over next door says he wants to make friends with you."

There was this twinkle in her eye. She said, "I love making friends. But if Mr. Uncle Ed Lee ever wants me to visit, he's gotta do something about that messy yard."

Now Miss Viola had a point. What she said was very true. So I told Uncle Ed Lee what Miss Viola said, and that old dude went right to work!

He picked up his trash . . .

and mowed his grass . . .

until he ran out of gas.

He even fixed the hanging
black shutters.

Later that afternoon, Miss Viola joined me by the mailbox.

"Look, Miss Viola!" I said. We couldn't believe our eyes. His place wasn't neat-neat, but it was much better than before.

Some of the yard was cut. No more trash was in the grass. And Uncle Ed Lee in a fresh bow tie set out a table and chairs, some lemonade, and a deck of playing cards.

Uncle Ed Lee then called us over. As only a good friend would, he poured lemonade for Miss Viola.

He poured me some too. Then we all sat down in the afternoon shade to enjoy a game of hearts.

Atheneum Books for Young Readers
An imprint of Simon & Schuster Children's Publishing Division
1230 Avenue of the Americas
New York, New York 10020

Text copyright © 1999 by Alice Faye Duncan
Illustrations copyright © 1999 by Catherine Stock

Book design by Michael Nelson

The text of this book is set in Wilke.
The illustrations are rendered in watercolor.

First Edition
Printed in Hong Kong
10 9 8 7 6 5 4 3 2 1

Library of Congress Cataloging-in-Publication Data
Duncan, Alice Faye.
Miss Viola and Uncle Ed Lee / by Alice Faye Duncan ; illustrated by Catherine Stock.—1st ed.
p.   cm.
Summary: A young boy helps his two neighbors, one as neat as a pin and the other as junky as a pack rat, become friends.
ISBN 0-689-80476-8
[1. Friendship—Fiction. 2. Old age—Fiction. 3. Orderliness—Fiction. 4. Afro-Americans—Fiction.] I. Stock, Catherine, ill. II. Title.
PZ7.D8947Mi   1999   [E]—dc20   95-30292   CIP   AC

FIRST
EDITION